BARBARA MAITLAND

MOO IN THE MORNING

PICTURES BY ANDREW KULMAN

BARBARA MAITLAND

MOO IN THE MORNING

PICTURES BY ANDREW KULMAN

HOUGHTON MIFFLIN   BOSTON

Here in the city,
the big, bright, busy city —

the big, bright, busy, NOISY city,

there are buses going BBLSH!

and cars going VROOM!

There are people slamming doors,

and voices calling "HEY!"

There's the garbage truck whirring,

crunching,

screeching,

tires squealing,

bells pealing.

4

There are clangings and clashes,
and rattles and rumbles
early in the morning.

Mom says it's loud here.
She likes city noise,
but not first thing.
Not so early in the morning.

She says we'll visit
Uncle Jack at his quiet
farm in the country.

In the day, the farm is fun.
There's a pond to swim in and a barn to hide in,

fields to play in and trees to climb.

But it's quiet and dark
when we go to bed —
how will we know when it's morning?

"Ooom-moooo!"
And again!
"Ooom-moooo!"
What's that?

It's a cow saying "MOOO!" in the morning!

14

Then the rooster crows,
"Cock-a-doodle-doo!"

And all the cows
moo in the morning.

A sleepy "Tweet,"

and all the birds sing

with a twitter and a chatter,

with the "Cock-a-doodle-doo!"
and the "Ooom-moooo!"
early in the morning.

19

Next to wake are the ducks and hens —

"Quack!" with a splash! and "Cluck, cluck, cluck!"

Ducks all quacking,

hens all clucking,

birds all tweeting,

rooster crowing,

and those mooers mooing in the morning.

The sheep wake "Baa!"
And the lambs wake "Bleat!"

"Baa!"

"Bleat!"

"Quack!"

"Cluck!"

"Tweet! Tweet! Tweet!"

"Cock-a-doodle-doo!"

And you-know-who going
"Moo, moo, MOOO!" in the morning.

Now the tractor is rumbling
and pots and pans are banging
and doors are slamming

and it's tweety, and quacky,
and clucky, and MOOEY
early in the morning.

Mom says it's time to go.
She likes the farm, but not that mooing
early in the morning.

Home in the city.
The big, bright, busy city.

24

The big, bright, busy, quiet city.